THE PATIO CLUB®

WRITTEN AND ILLUSTRATED BY
CARYN MOTTILLA

I0550621

May's
Happy Moments

May's Happy Moments
The Patio Club®
Published by Open Window Publishing
Castle Rock, CO

Publisher's Cataloging-in-Publication data

Names: Mottilla, Caryn, author.
Title: April showers and fools / by Caryn Mottilla.
Description: First trade paperback original edition. Also available as an ebook. | Castle Rock [Colorado] : Open Window Publishing, 2019. | Series: The Patio Club.
Identifiers: ISBN 978-0-9997471-5-5
Subjects: LCSH: Old age—Fiction. | May's Happy Moments—Fiction. | Aging parents—Fiction. | Short stories.
BISAC: FICTION / General.
Classification: LCC PS374.O43 | DDC 813–dc22

Cover design by Caryn Mottilla

QUANTITY PURCHASES: Schools, companies, professional groups, clubs, and other organizations may qualify for special terms when ordering quantities of this title. For information, email ThePatioClub@gmail.com.

OPEN WINDOW
PUBLISHING

The Patio Club® is dedicated to the men and women in assisted living communities, memory and Hospice care who have listened to the adventures of The Patio Club®. They expressed their hope for these stories to be published and shared with others across the country.

Introducing the Patio Club

The Patio Club was originally formed by two sets of sisters—Elaine and Adele from New Jersey, and Betty and Mildred from Kentucky. The women were young when they met in the 1940s. The years passed by, and later in life, the four adventurous women made a pact that after they died they would meet up and visit retirement and assisted living communities. After they passed away, they came to Happy Visions Retirement Home and liked it so much they decided to stay.

The women call themselves "The Patio Club," because they sit outside on the patio of Happy Visions. Each day, Elaine, Adele,

Betty and Mildred are surrounded by colorful sparkles, and they meet a steady stream of interesting visitors and residents who pass through Happy Visions on their way to unknown destinations.

One amazing thing is that the Patio Club can look to the sky and watch a video of each person's life. This precious gift lets the Patio Club understand the unique story that each person carries with them.

May's Happy Moments

IT WAS EARLY IN THE MONTH OF MAY, and a cool breeze blew as the women of the Patio Club sat outside after dinner. Elaine, Adele, Betty and Mildred watched as several residents of Happy Visions Retirement Home came outside one last time before putting another day to rest.

Betty watched the residents with interest and said, "It seems to me that most of the residents lose their energy after dinner. They look like they are thinking about something."

Elaine smiled and said, "Maybe they are eating too much dessert after dinner! Too much sugar can bring you down."

Adele and Mildred smiled at Elaine's comment because everyone knew how much Elaine loved dessert!

At that moment, the screen door opened one last time and a tall woman named May was the last resident to come outside. Mildred said, "I wonder if May was born in the month of May and that's why she carries that name."

May continued walking slowly across the patio. In her arms, she carried a blue and white quilt. She sat on a chair with a bright orange cushion that the maintenance crew had put out earlier that day.

As the sun was setting, May took her seat and spread the colorful quilt over her legs. Adele watched May closely and said, "It's a funny thing. When I see May early in the morning, she is often sitting on the front porch and her bright smile says she is happy."

"I agree," said Elaine. "She loves watching the birds and listening to them as they greet another day of life. However, I often notice that after the evening meal, May seems withdrawn. From the look on her face, it's as though she is a million miles away."

Betty looked at the other residents on the patio. She said, "In fact, most of the residents seem the same way later in the day. I wonder what happens to change their mood."

Mildred said, "A breathtaking sunset is coloring the sky a rich purple and pink. In spite of the beauty of nature all around us, I also wonder what happens to the residents late in the day."

Adele said, "My guess is maybe they miss their spouses and companions at that time. There is nothing to distract them from missing those they love."

Adele continued and said, "I remember when Johnny passed away. He had been my husband and companion

for so many years. After he died, I watched soap operas during the day to occupy my time. In the evening, however, I had more time to think about how much I missed him."

Elaine said, "I remember when Will passed away. I found a group that travelled. We sure had some great times. No matter how many years have passed since then, I still miss Will—especially in the evening."

Betty laughed and said, "When Richard died, I was so mad! We spent many years annoyed with each other and fighting. Right when it seemed life got easier for us, he was gone! I wasted so many moments being annoyed with him when I could have been happy instead. Maybe missing our loved ones is really a way to stay connected to them."

Mildred thoughtfully listened to the comments of Adele, Elaine and Betty. "Maybe in the evening, May misses her husband, Charles. I heard he passed away not long after he and May moved into Happy Visions. I sure wish May could carry the happiness she feels each

morning all day long."

The women watched May stand up and fold her quilt with great care. Her unique quilt appeared to be handmade. It had the initials, M&C, in each square.

Betty saw the initials and said, "I'll bet the initials stand for May and Charles. That quilt looks like it has been around for quite a few years."

As the moon appeared in the evening sky, all of the residents began leaving the patio. Soft white sparkles swirled around them as they went back to their rooms to get ready for bed.

The screen door closed one last time. Suddenly Adele said, "I have an idea! Let's help May carry the happiness she feels in the morning through to the evening, as well."

Adele spoke softly, "I noticed several bluebirds on the back of her quilt. Let's ask a bluebird to visit May tomorrow morning when she's having her coffee on the porch. You might laugh at this, but I believe if you ask a bluebird, one will find her."

Betty said, "Who are we to laugh at this? We are surrounded every day by colorful sparkles! Asking a bluebird seems like a good idea!"

The next morning, May followed her usual routine and sat outside drinking coffee. Walter the retirement home dog joined her. He slowly laid down at May's feet, and his bushy tail covered her pink slippers.

A big smile crossed May's face as she petted Walter's head and said, "Did you come outside to birdwatch with me sweetie? It sure is a beautiful day."

As May sipped her coffee, a pastel-colored bluebird landed on the porch railing in front of her. "You, must be the bluebird of happiness," she said to the beautiful bird.

"I hope you are here to stay!" The bluebird tilted its head and made no attempt to fly away.

The day continued to unfold, and several of the residents noticed May seemed happier. She chatted easily with other residents at lunch. She even joined them for Bingo in the afternoon!

After the evening meal, the Patio Club heard May invite her friend, Edith, to sit outside to watch the sunset. "I'll bring my quilt, so we won't catch a chill," said May.

Elaine, Adele, Betty and Mildred watched with joy. "You see," said Betty, "happiness comes when you live in the now!"

Mildred heard her sister Betty's comment. "Why, Betty, Mom was always telling you to pay attention to the present moment. She would be so proud of you for finally understanding what she tried for over twenty years to teach you!" Betty and the others laughed at Mildred's warm acknowledgment.

After dinner, May walked onto the patio with Edith. May unfolded her blue and white quilt and offered part of it to Edith. As she did this, a warm evening breeze swept softly across their faces.

A picnic table was on the patio near Edith and May. As the women sat down, the same bluebird from earlier that morning landed on the picnic table. May smiled and winked at the bluebird as though they had a secret.

Adele watched May and said, "Do you think May will realize it's the same bluebird we sent to her earlier this morning? It's a great reminder to be aware that happiness is often found right in front of you."

"May definitely looks happier tonight," said Mildred. "She is smiling and sharing her lovely quilt with Edith. That may be the secret to happiness—enjoying the very moment in which we are living."

After the sun disappeared from the sky, cool evening air descended onto the patio. Residents began heading

back inside to their rooms. Elaine, Adele, Betty and Mildred watched as a light came on in May's room and she began getting ready for bed.

"I know," said Elaine. "Let's look to the video in the sky to see if we can find the story of May's quilt. It certainly seems special to her."

The women of the Patio Club stood together and pictured May's beautiful quilt. Suddenly, the colorful video lit up the sky and began to play.

The four women were delighted to see May and her husband, Charles, when they were young lovers. They were sitting outside on a front porch swing at May's house.

Mildred said, "It seems May and Charles were teenagers when they began to call themselves boyfriend and girlfriend."

The video continued and Charles handed May a brightly colored gift-wrapped box with a big purple bow on it. He said, "Happy Birthday, May!"

May unwrapped the box and inside was the blue and white quilt May still carries with her each day. "What a beautiful quilt, Charles. Thank you so much!"

Just then, Charles bent down and kissed May on her cheek. May joked, "I hope my parents are not watching us through the window!"

May inspected her new gift and slowly turned it over. On the back of the quilt was a picture of bluebirds flying against a cloudy gray sky. Underneath the picture, stitched into the quilt, was a special message from Charles just for her. It read:

"Even though skies are sometimes gray, the bluebird of happiness is always closer than you realize. Love, Charles."

Charles smiled and said to May, "I want you to keep this special quilt with you when I am not around. Whenever you miss me, just wrap the quilt around you and pretend

it's me hugging you."

"Wasn't it a great idea to send the bluebird this morning to May?" said Adele. "I got the idea when I saw bluebirds on May's quilt last evening. I was hoping she would take it as a sign that Charles still watches over her."

The video continued and May sat talking to her childhood friend Pat. May gave more history about the quilt and said, "I held onto my birthday quilt when Charles served in the Vietnam war. When he left the service, I slept with the quilt whenever Charles traveled for work as we raised our small family."

May told Pat back then, "I loved this quilt so much. One day, I decided to make quilts with women from my church. We always had so much fun while we worked and laughed together. When the quilts were finished, we gave them to Charles, and he delivered the quilts we had made to veterans at the VA hospital.

The women of the Patio Club were completely enchanted by the video and the present moment. Mildred said, "The quilt she carries with her each morning and evening has a long history of love behind it. What happiness that quilt still brings May each day."

The video came to an end as the light in May's room went out. Later that same night, Elaine, Adele, Betty and Mildred looked in on May. She was sleeping peacefully, covered with the quilt Charles had given her so long ago.

The following morning, there wasn't a cloud in the deep blue sky. As usual, May sat on the front porch drinking her coffee. Her new friend Edith joined her. The women sat, watching bluebirds crisscrossing in the air like they were in a parade.

May was wrapped snuggly in her colorful quilt. Without a word, May removed the quilt from her shoulders and shared part of it with Edith.

The four women of the Patio Club were nearby smiling

and watching all of this. Suddenly, May said excitedly to Edith, "I have an idea! Let's make you a happiness quilt! It should take us a few weeks, if we work together. We would have so much fun!"

Edith looked young again as she answered May, "I'd love for you to help me make a happiness quilt! We have to be sure and put bluebirds of happiness on it. There is no better way to live in the now than by making a quilt with a dear friend."

Adele watched the women from a short distance away. She smiled and said, "It's amazing how easily happiness blesses new and old friendships. The moments spent with friends seem so much sweeter than time spent alone. AND, of course, making a good quilt always brings happiness!"

MAY you be blessed with happiness and friendship today.

With love from the Patio Club.

The end.

The Patio Club's Story

IN NOVEMBER OF 2016, I began writing fictional stories for retirement and assisted living communities. This occurred because of a simple request from an older gentleman in his 80s who asked if I could write a story about people "their age." Writing and telling stories has always come easily to me. I happily said , "yes." I was excited at the challenge and have written a story each month since then. They are about a fictional retirement/ assisted living community named *Happy Visions*. Each month I read to retirement and assisted living communities. The joy of doing this is overwhelming.

In July of 2017, I was reading to a group of older women as they sat outside *on the patio* in the shade. The women's ages reached up to 95. When I left the patio that day, I decided at that moment to write a story for them called "The Patio Club." The series began with that story.

The stories I write come effortlessly to me. It is as if I am divinely inspired. As I began writing the first story in the Patio Club series, I was so surprised as I watched the story come to life. It is the story of two sets of sisters, Elaine and Adele from New Jersey, and Mildred and Betty from Kentucky. They made a pact that when they died they would meet up and visit retirement and assisted living communities.

Imagine my surprise—because in real life Elaine and Adele (sisters) were my aunts from New Jersey, and Betty (my mother) and Mildred (my aunt) were sisters from Kentucky! My Aunt Mildred was the last one to join The Patio Club. She passed away earlier in 2017. The Patio Club™ stories now touch people from around the country and hopefully someday from around the world.

My dream is that The Patio Club™ series will be read to the people in assisted living, memory and Hospice care communities. As I read each month to these special people, I realized that it is often difficult to visit loved ones who are in the assisted living population. What I have found is that reading a story seems to transform everyone from the reader to the listener. I have seen people with all kinds of health challenges perk up when listening to the joyful adventures of The Patio Club™. They are in the present moment as they listen and during that time there is nothing wrong with them.

My wish is that people will take the adventure of reading a story (about 12 to 15 minutes) from The Patio Club Series to a loved one. It will transform the visit from one where it may be difficult to find something to talk about, to one where both the reader and listener are moved beyond words.

With gratitude and love,

- Caryn

Acknowledgments

THE PATIO CLUB is dedicated to my aunts Elaine, Adele, Mildred, and my mother Betty. Although the characters in the Patio Club are fictional, they are based on these important women who impacted my life.

Special thanks to my sons Carson and Cooper, as well as, family and friends who have listened to these stories. They have enthusiastically cheered for me to follow my dream to write and illustrate stories that bring joy and adventure to the lives of others.

Finally, I am grateful to God for the gifts He has given me to serve the people in assisted living, memory and Hospice care.

About the Author

CARYN BEGAN WRITING children's stories for her children in the 1990s. In 2016, as she read children's stories to assisted living communities, residents asked her to write a story "for people their age." That was how the adventure of writing for the adult and assisted population began.

Since that time, Caryn has written a monthly series called The Patio Club®. It takes place at a retirement home/assisted living community named Happy

Visions. The Patio Club™ are the first stories published by Caryn for that age group. The stories have captured the attention of people of all ages across the country.

The Patio Club™ stories are a bridge between the reader and the listener. Family and friends that visit assisted living, memory and Hospice care communities may struggle for something to talk about. Reading a story like The Patio Club™ to these special residents takes them on an adventure without them ever having to leave the room. It creates an opening for some interesting conversations!

Caryn lives in Colorado. She has two grown sons, Carson and Cooper